# DRACULA'S DAUGHTER

# Crabtree Publishing Company
## www.crabtreebooks.com

PMB 16A, 350 Fifth Avenue,
Suite 3308,
New York, NY 10118

616 Welland Avenue,
St. Catharines, Ontario
Canada, L2M 5V6

Hoffman, Mary, 1945-
    Dracula's daughter / written by Mary Hoffman; illustrated by Chris Riddell.
       p. cm. -- (Yellow bananas)
    Summary: A family adopt the baby on their doorstep and enjoy bringing her
up, though her teeth grow in sharp and pointed until Dracula comes to claim
her for his own.
    ISBN-13: 978-0-7787-0954-1 (rlb)
    ISBN-10: 0-7787-0954-X (rlb)
    ISBN-13: 978-0-7787-1000-4 (pbk)
    ISBN-10: 0-7787-1000-9 (pbk)
    [1. Dracula, Count (Fictitious character)--Fiction. 2. Halloween--Fiction.]
I. Riddell, Chris, ill. II. Title. III. Series.
    PZ7.H67562Dr 2006
    [E]--dc22

                                                              2005035769

                                                                  LC

Published by Crabtree Publishing in 2006
First published in 1988 by Egmont Books Ltd.
Text copyright © Mary Hoffman 1988
Illustrations © Chris Riddell 1988
The Author and Illustrator have asserted their moral rights.
Paperback ISBN 0-7787-1000-9
Reinforced Hardcover Binding ISBN 0-7787-0954-X

# Mary Hoffman

# DRACULA'S DAUGHTER

## Illustrated by Chris Riddell

 YELLOW BANANAS

*For Ertaç and the*
*other Lea Valley juniors who*
*encouraged me to finish it*
*M.H.*


*For Katy*
*C.R.*

# Chapter One

ANGELA WAS A model child in every way. Of
course her arrival was unusual. Mr. and Mrs.
Batty were not expecting a baby – they were
expecting a parcel of plants they had ordered
for the garden. So they weren't surprised when
there was a ring at the doorbell and a basket
dumped on the step. Only in the basket was a
baby girl with brown eyes and black hair. Mr.
and Mrs. Batty forgot all about the plants and
looked after the baby instead.

She looked like a little angel, so they decided
to call her Angela. On the first anniversary of

her arrival through the mail, the baby was
adopted and became Angela Batty. There were
no problems for the first few years. She walked
and talked on time, ate up her greens, tidied up
after her games, and did not pull the cat's tail.

The trouble really began on her fifth birthday.
In the bundle with Angela there had been an
envelope saying:

*"This child was born on October 31st. Open this letter on her 5th birthday."*

Of course, Mr. and Mrs. Batty had wanted to open the envelope right away, in case it contained a clue about her parents, but they somehow felt it would be unlucky to look inside before the given date. So after Angela's birthday party, when all her friends had gone home clutching their loot bags, her parents solemnly took down the envelope and opened it.

Thank you for looking
after my daughter. You
will be hearing from
me Clara du Plotin

That was all. Mr. and Mrs. Batty were a bit disappointed and they objected to the writer referring to Angela as "her" daughter.

"She's ours now – it's all legal," said Mrs. Batty firmly.

"Besides," said her husband, "if she was a rich lady, as it seems, why did she have to go dumping her child on a doorstep?"

For a while everything went on as normal. Angela went to school, made friends, and was called a good girl by her teachers. Several of her friends began to get loose teeth and talk about the tooth fairy. So Angela's parents were not surprised when she got her first gap. But, when the new tooth grew to fill the gap, they *were* a bit worried. All the other children had nice square teeth, but Angela's came to a sharp

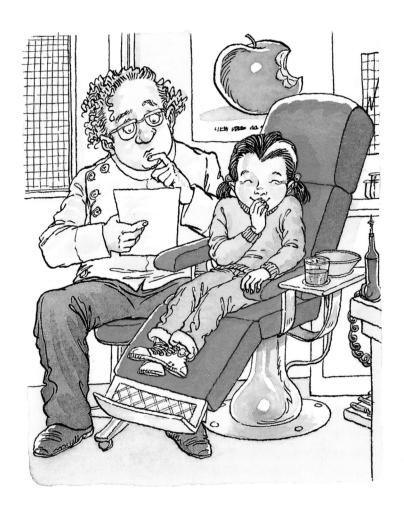

point, like a shark's. The dentist was confused,
but not really worried – he said Angela's teeth
could be filed straight when she was older. But
even he declared himself beaten by the time
Angela had a mouthful of sharp pointed teeth.

Some of Angela's old friends were no longer allowed to come and play at her house, their parents didn't like the look of those fangs.

Other odd things had started to happen too. Angela had always been good about eating her vegetables, but now she became almost entirely a meat-eater. She loved hamburgers, pork chops, roasts, and steaks if she could get them. She would happily eat the kinds of meat that other children didn't enjoy, like liver and kidney. She also enjoyed beets, black currant juice, red cabbage, and raspberries.

When Mr. and Mrs. Batty saw their beloved daughter lifting her smiling face from a bowlful of raspberries, with her pointed teeth stained all red, they exchanged nervous looks.

Other strange things happened too. Mrs. Batty took a course in French cookery and began to be adventurous about sauces. But the day she came home with her first bunch of garlic,

Angela let out a scream and hid in the garden shed. She wouldn't come back inside until Mrs. Batty had thrown the garlic out. The Battys did not have Angela christened as a baby and now they were beginning to wonder if that would help. They invited the minister over one afternoon. All went well until Angela came in from school. She took one look at his collar and cross and ran for the shed again.

The mystery was settled once and for all that evening. After Angela had gone to bed, Mr. and Mrs. Batty got out the envelope and read the card inside it again. Mr. Batty had been doing the crossword in the newspaper and now he pointed to the signature with a shaking finger.

"My dear – it's an anagram. Mix up the letters in CLARA DU COTUN and what do you get? COUNT DRACULA!"

## Chapter Two

IT DIDN'T TAKE the Battys long to get used
to having a vampire in the family. After all,
Angela didn't show any signs of wanting to bite
anyone. But one thing her parents had definitely
decided was that if her birth father ever *did*
turn up, they would not let him take her
away from them.

"If she *is* a vampire," said Mrs. Batty, which
was a thing she never talked about except to
Mr. Batty, "at least if she stays with us she will
be a nice well brought up vampire, who brushes
her teeth after every meal."

But the teeth weren't the only problem. It was an unusually warm fall and the Battys left the bedroom windows open all night to cool the house down. One night Mr. Batty could not sleep because of the heat and he went to look in on Angela. He was back in his own bedroom in a flash, shaking his wife awake.

"Wake up, my dear!" he shouted, "she's gone! Angela's not there!"

But when Mrs. Batty woke up and ran down the hallway, she found Angela sleeping peacefully in her bed, with her usual angelic smile.

"You must have been dreaming," she told her husband angrily, "waking me up and frightening me for nothing like that!" But she closed Angela's window all the same.

October was as warm as September and the Battys began to prepare for Angela's seventh birthday party. She had asked for a Halloween party, with dressing up, a cauldron cake, and jack-o'-lanterns in the windows. Her parents were nervous – it seemed to them to be asking for trouble. On the other hand, lots of normal children were going to Halloween parties too.

"It's bound to appeal to her nature," said Mr. Batty. "Angela being what we think she is. But she's a good girl. I don't think she can be *all* vampire, you know."

Angela certainly looked all
vampire on the night. She
wore a short black
cloak that Mrs. Batty
had made for her,
and had circled her
eyes with red
lipstick. She had
rubbed green eye
shadow – bought
specially – all
over her face.
When she smiled
her fangy little
smile, her parents
couldn't help shuddering.

"I hope we're doing the right
thing with this party," said
Mrs. Batty, as Angela rushed
to open the door. She let
in another vampire, two
witches, an imp, and
a wizard.

"You look terrific, Angela!" said one of the
witches, who was her friend Emma from
school, "Really scary!"

After they were joined by some more vampires and a ghost or two, the party really got going. As the games were played and prizes won, most of the children acquired long red fingernails or white plastic fangs. Angela began to look just like everyone else. The house had a jack-o'-lantern in every window and even Mrs. Batty wore a tall black hat. So they were visited by an especially large number of trick-or-treat gangs that night. Mrs. Batty was prepared, with a big bowl of currant cookies she had made, right by the front door.

So when the doorbell rang yet again, she already had a cookie in her hand as she opened the door to a tall black-haired man in an opera cloak, who looked just like Count Dracula.

# Chapter Three

"GOOD EVENING!" SAID the man who looked like Count Dracula. "Can I come in?"

Mrs. Batty stood frozen in the hall, the cookie in her hand. Just then her husband popped his head out of the living room.

"Oh good," he said, "I see the entertainer's here. Dressed for the part too! Come in then Mr. . . . er?"

"Count," said the man.

"Mr. Count," said Mr. Batty, "the children are all ready for you."

"Mr. Count" gave a ghastly smile and walked into the Batty's living room. Mrs. Batty watched silently in horror, unable to move or speak. The cat streaked through the hall and out through the front door. Mrs. Batty automatically closed it and went into the living room. The children were excited about the entertainer.

"Hey, Angela," said her friend Darren, "he looks just like the real thing! Watch out for your neck!"

The entertainer didn't tell jokes or do tricks.

But whenever he spoke or looked at the children they cheered and laughed. All except Angela. She was watching him with a strange look in her eye. And Mrs. Batty was watching her.

"Mr. Count" was watching everyone. He hadn't thought it would be so hard to recognize his own daughter, but all these little humans looked like vampires to him.

When he said, "Who wants to come with me to my castle?" all the children put up their hands and shouted "Me! Me!" Except one. And that one really *did* look like a vampire – the teeth were very natural, even though all that green stuff was obviously fake.

The doorbell rang again. Mrs. Batty saw the tall dark stranger moving towards her beloved daughter and felt something snap inside her. "Angela!" she shrieked as she rushed between them.

The man turned on her with flashing eyes and fangs bared. He looked as if he was going to sink them into her plump pink neck. The children went very quiet and then there was a

rustling sound. Angela
had spread out her arms
under her black cloak
and flapped steadily
up to the ceiling.

The "entertainer"
took his eyes off Mrs.
Batty to watch his
daughter proudly as
she swooped
around the room.
Mr. Batty was
nowhere to be
seen. Mrs. Batty
picked up a
plastic sword that
the "wizard" had
brought and held it
upside down in the
shape of a cross,
right in front of the
man in the black cloak.

"If only I had some garlic," she muttered.

"Come down, Fangella!" called the tall dark man. "I've come to take you home. I see you are a credit to me."

"Over my dead body!" cried Mrs. Batty angrily, waving the plastic sword.

The man flinched, but said menacingly, "That could be arranged."

"Oh no you don't," said Angela firmly, hanging upside down from the ceiling lamp.

"I don't want to go to your horrid damp old castle with its spiders and rats. I want to stay here, where there's central heating and a nice cuddly cat."

"But Fangella, you are my daughter!"

"Don't you dare call her that," yelled Mrs. Batty. "Her name is *Angela* and she is my daughter now! She's adopted." She took the adoption certificate, which she always carried in her pocket and waved it in the tall man's face, never letting go of the sword.

"She's not a Dopted, she's a Vampire!" shouted the man. "I left her here nearly seven years ago, when I – er – had to go away for a while. And now I've come back to collect her."

"I'm not going," said Angela. "You tried to bite my mother!"

The man gave a nasty laugh.

"I *did* bite your mother, Fangella, long ago. She was another one just like this, but she turned out to be too tough for me."

Angela gasped. "You mean I'm only *half a vampire?*"

"Yes, but your mother got away when I stole you and found some other human to help her. Between them they had me followed and locked up in a crypt with a strong spell on the door. I couldn't escape until your mother died. She never found out where I left you and now I claim you as my own. It's a vampire's father that really matters – by the way, where *is* that silly human that thought I was a party magician?"

Angela looked around wildly for Mr. Batty but he wasn't there. The other children were all looking up at Angela on the ceiling with their mouths open.

"I'm not going," said Angela again. "I'm only
half a vampire and I'm going to choose to be
the other half."

"We'll see about that," said the tall man. "Just you wait until I get my fangs on you." Then he spread his cloak and aimed himself at the lamp.

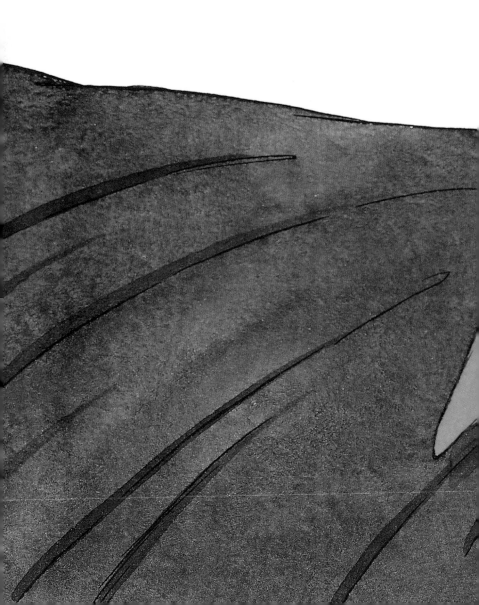

## Chapter Four

AS HE LAUNCHED himself up toward Angela,
the man in black suddenly gave a loud scream
and fell to the ground at the sight of Mr. Batty
in the doorway, holding a large tree with
orange berries on its branches and earth
dropping from its roots. Behind him stood
another tall man.

"Gotcha, you crazy old bat!" said Mr. Batty triumphantly, and prodded the cloaked figure with the tree. The shrieks and moans became louder. "We don't want you or any of your kind ever coming to bother our Angela again! This is a rowan tree and I know you vampires can't bear them. I'm going down to the garden center tomorrow to buy up their whole stock and I'm going to plant them all around the house!

Now be off with you!" Mr. Batty motioned to the window and Mrs. Batty opened it.

The man who looked just like Count Dracula dragged himself up onto the window ledge and sat hunched there with his black cloak drooping down like a tattered old umbrella.

"So this is all the thanks I get," he hissed up at Angela. "A fine vampire you've turned out to be!"

"Half vampire," corrected Angela, still upside down.

"Very well," he said, "stay here and
eat your rice pudding and go to
Sunday school and knit the cat a
pair of socks if that's what you want.
You'll never get another chance like this.
You would have had a much more exciting
life with me!" Then he launched himself out of
the window and flapped away into the night.
Angela landed neatly on the floor right side
up and gave a bow.

"Come on, dear," whispered Mr. Batty, putting down his tree and starting to clap. Mrs. Batty got the message and clapped loudly. Soon all the children were clapping and cheering wildly.

"That was really *wicked*, Angela," said Darren admiringly. "How did you do the flying part? And who *was* that geezer?"

"Oh, just a distant relation on a flying visit," giggled Angela.

"I'll never forget tonight," said Mrs. Batty, when the guests had all gone home and she and her husband were drinking their cocoa.

"When did you realize he wasn't the entertainer?"

"When I let the real one in, of course," said Mr. Batty. "He caught on really quickly and helped me dig up the rowan."

"That *was* lucky," said Mrs. Batty. "I didn't know we had a rowan tree in the garden."

"We didn't," said Mr. Batty grimly, "I stole it from the garden next door. I believe they'll think it was the trick-or-treaters."

"Well it will be hard to explain why you did it," said his wife. "But I'm really proud of you – and of Angela."

"And I'm proud of you honey, facing that old Count with nothing but a plastic sword."

"You know one thing though, dear," said Mrs. Batty, "he made me think it might be a bit dull for Angela living with us. We *are* a bit set in our ways."

"Still, she chose us didn't she?" said her husband, licking the cocoa froth from his lips. "She can't think we're too boring. But I'll try to be more adventurous if you like. What do you want me to do?"

"How about a nice vacation?" asked Mrs. Batty. "We could go somewhere a bit different for Christmas."

Mr. Batty smiled. "All right, dear. You get some brochures and we'll take our Angela off to somewhere exotic. Only be careful – nowhere near Transylvania!"

 **YeLLow Bananas**

## Other titles in the
## Yellow Banana bunch:

Story  Facts  Activities
Go Bananas

## Other titles in
## Yellow Go Bananas:

**The Reluctant Rajput**

**Speak Up, Spike!**

**Cuda of the Celts**

**Tara's Tree House**